Full of adventure and lessons, Honey in the Woods Reading & Coloring Books are fun and educational tools to expand vocabulary, introduce foreign language and encourage creativity. Take this journey with Honey as she discovers that a day in the woods is full of surprises.

Remember to:

- ☐ Read
- ☐ Color
- ☐ Say underlined words aloud
- ☐ Find and count hidden shapes, numbers and letters

Let's make learning fun!

HONEY IN THE WOODS

A Coloring Story

By Miso Agogo

Illustrations by Kade Norman

This book belongs to:

_____

Print name here

_____

Sign name here

Once upon a dream, there
were three <u>osos</u> who lived
deep inside the woods.
But they were bored and
wanted friends to play with.

*osos means bears

SISTER BEAR

BROTHER BEAR

BABY BEAR

Meanwhile, there was a
little <u>niña</u> by the name of
Honey. She went into the
woods alone in search
of the perfect flower for
her mother.

*niña means girl

HONEY

While searching through
the woods, Honey walked
onto the porch of a
cute cottage.

"Hello, my name is Honey.
I saw your roses.
May I pick some as a gift
for my mother?"

"Sure! Come on in,"
said Baby Bear.

Honey entered the house and followed Baby Bear.

"Would you like to be <u>amigos</u>?" he asked.

"I have never been anyone's amigo before. What is that?" asked Honey.

"Amigo is the Spanish word for friend. And after I find a basket, I'll help you pick flowers," said Baby Bear.

Baby Bear found the basket and was ready to pick flowers.

"I'm getting hungry. Do you have anything to eat?" asked Honey.

Baby Bear grabbed two spoons. They sat on the kitchen floor and ate the entire tub of ice cream.

"I feel awful now," said Honey. "Where are your parents?"

"They're never home," said Baby Bear.

"You may not have your parents, but now you have a friend," said Honey.

Then Baby Bear led Honey to his parents' room where they watched cartoons, laughed and soon fell asleep.

Meanwhile, Sister and Brother Bear received a call from Mother Bear.

"It will be a thirty-day journey before we return home, so take care of each other until we get back. If you find any honey in the woods, eat it."

Sister and Brother Bear
stood outside their <u>padres</u>
room hungry.

"Well, that little girl's name
is Honey, and she *does*
look sweet," said Brother
Bear.

"Mama wasn't talking
about *that* kind of honey,"
said Sister Bear.

"Of course not, but
I'm bored. Let's scare
them anyway," said
Brother Bear.

*padres means parents

Brother and Sister Bear slowly entered Mother and Father Bear's room, but they did not see Honey nor Baby Bear. The kids had jumped out the window with their baskets to finally pick flowers.

Just as Baby Bear put a
yellow rose in Honey's hair,
Brother and Sister Bear
came charging towards
them with claws extended
and saliva dripping from
their teeth. Baby Bear had
never seen this look before.

"iCorrer!" Baby Bear shouted to Honey in fear for her life.

Honey was confused as the bears quickly approached. She could not understand what Baby Bear was saying. But the look on their faces frightened her. So she dropped the basket and ran as fast as she could — all the way home.

*correr means run

Honey was so upset
because her mother
warned her about
wandering off alone and
talking to strangers;
yet she was more
disappointed because she
didn't get all the flowers
she wanted for her mother.
And she wondered if she
would ever see her only
friend again...

- How do you think this story ends?

- Why did Honey show up at Baby Bear's house?

- Why did the bears run after Honey?

- How do you think Honey feels when Baby Bear tells her to run from Brother and Sister Bear?

- Why did Honey not understand what Baby Bear was yelling?

Words I Learned Today

Definition - What a word means

Pronunciation - (How a word sounds)

Spanish Words	Sounds Like	Means
hola	oh-lah	hello
osos	oh-so-s	bears
niña	neen-ya	girl
amigos	ah-me-go-s	friends
padres	pah-drays	parents
correr	core-err	run

English Words

cot•tage (cot-tedge) - a one-level house or cabin, usually in a rural setting, like a forest

jour•ney (jur-nee) - traveling from one place to another

ex•tend•ed (x-sten-ded) - increased in length; made larger or longer

dis•ap•point•ed (dis-a-point-ed) - sad or displeased, because something didn't work out as planned

Tell Us What You Think!

Reviews, questions and comments are always welcome. Remember to like us on Facebook at Honey in the Woods Reading & Coloring Books.

Let's make learning fun!

CPSIA information can be obtained
at www.ICGtesting.com
Printed in the USA
LVHW020843170520
655785LV00011B/577